A **4D** BOOK

ADVENTURES IN MAKERSPACE

A PHOTO JOURNAL MISSION

WRITTEN BY
SHANNON MCCLINTOCK MILLER
AND
BLAKE HOENA

ILLUSTRATED BY
ALAN BROWN

STONE ARCH BOOKS
a capstone imprint

capstone®

www.mycapstone.com

A *Photo Journal Mission* is published by Stone Arch Books,
a Capstone imprint
1710 Roe Crest Drive, North Mankato, Minnesota 56003
www.mycapstonepub.com

Library of Congress Cataloging-in-Publication Data
Names: Miller, Shannon (Shannon McClintock), author. | Hoena, B. A., author.
  | Brown, Alan (Illustrator), illustrator.
Title: A photo journal mission / by Shannon McClintock Miller and Blake Hoena
  ; illustrated by Alan Brown.
Description: North Mankato, Minnesota : Stone Arch Books, [2019] | Series:
  Adventures in makerspace | Audience: Ages 8-10.
Identifiers: LCCN 2018044116| ISBN 9781496579508 (hardcover) | ISBN
  9781496579546 (pbk.) | ISBN 9781496579584 (ebook pdf)
Subjects: LCSH: Scrapbook journaling--Juvenile literature. | Diaries--Juvenile
  literature. | Makerspaces--Juvenile literature. | LCGFT: Graphic novels.
Classification: LCC PN245 .M55 2019 | DDC 745.593/8--dc23 LC record
  available at https://lccn.loc.gov/2018044116

Book design and art direction: Mighty Media
Editorial direction: Kellie M. Hultgren
Music direction: Elizabeth Draper
Music written and produced by Mark Mallman

Printed and bound in the United States of America
PA48

CONTENTS

1. Ask an adult to download the app.  Capstone 4D Education

2. Scan any page with the star.

3. Enjoy your cool stuff!

—— OR ——

Use this password at capstone4D.com

photo.79508

MEET THE SPECIALIST

ABILITIES:
speed reader, tech titan, foreign language master, traveler through literature and history

MS. GILLIAN
TEACHER-LIBRARIAN

MEET THE STUDENTS

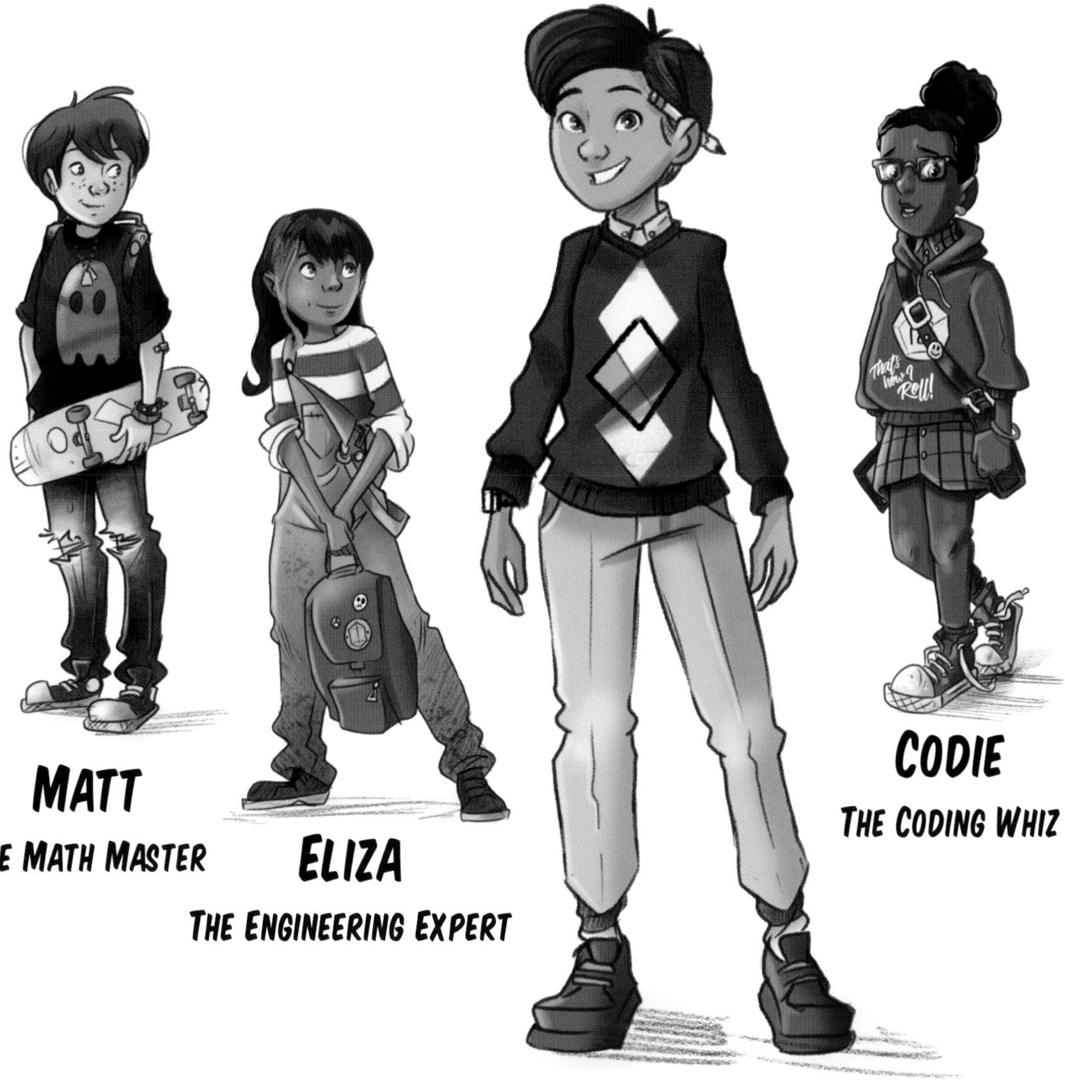

That's how I Roll!

MATT
THE MATH MASTER

ELIZA
THE ENGINEERING EXPERT

CYRUS
THE SCIENCE GENIUS

CODIE
THE CODING WHIZ

JOURNAL ASSIGNMENT

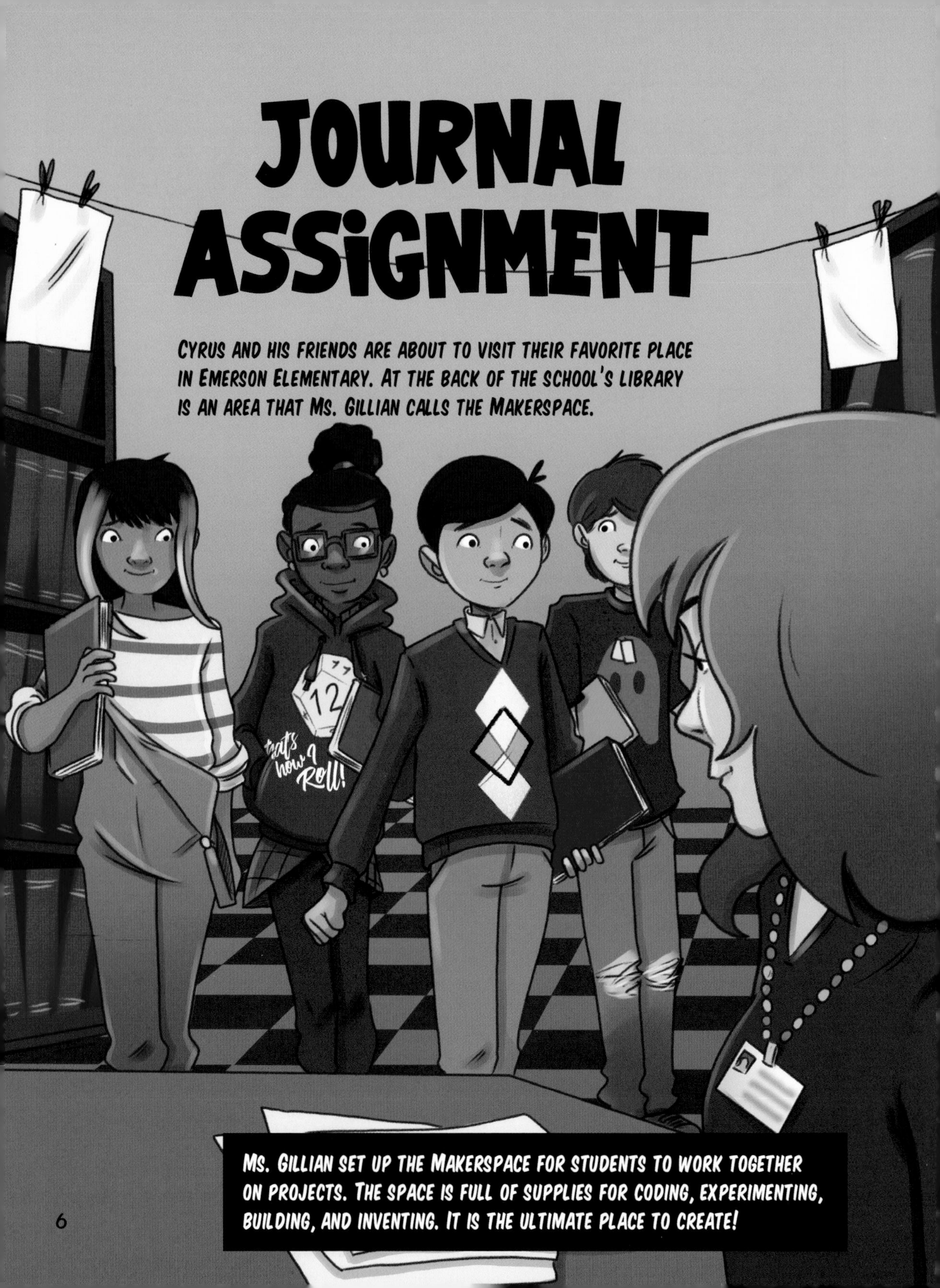
CYRUS AND HIS FRIENDS ARE ABOUT TO VISIT THEIR FAVORITE PLACE IN EMERSON ELEMENTARY. AT THE BACK OF THE SCHOOL'S LIBRARY IS AN AREA THAT MS. GILLIAN CALLS THE MAKERSPACE.
MS. GILLIAN SET UP THE MAKERSPACE FOR STUDENTS TO WORK TOGETHER ON PROJECTS. THE SPACE IS FULL OF SUPPLIES FOR CODING, EXPERIMENTING, BUILDING, AND INVENTING. IT IS THE ULTIMATE PLACE TO CREATE!

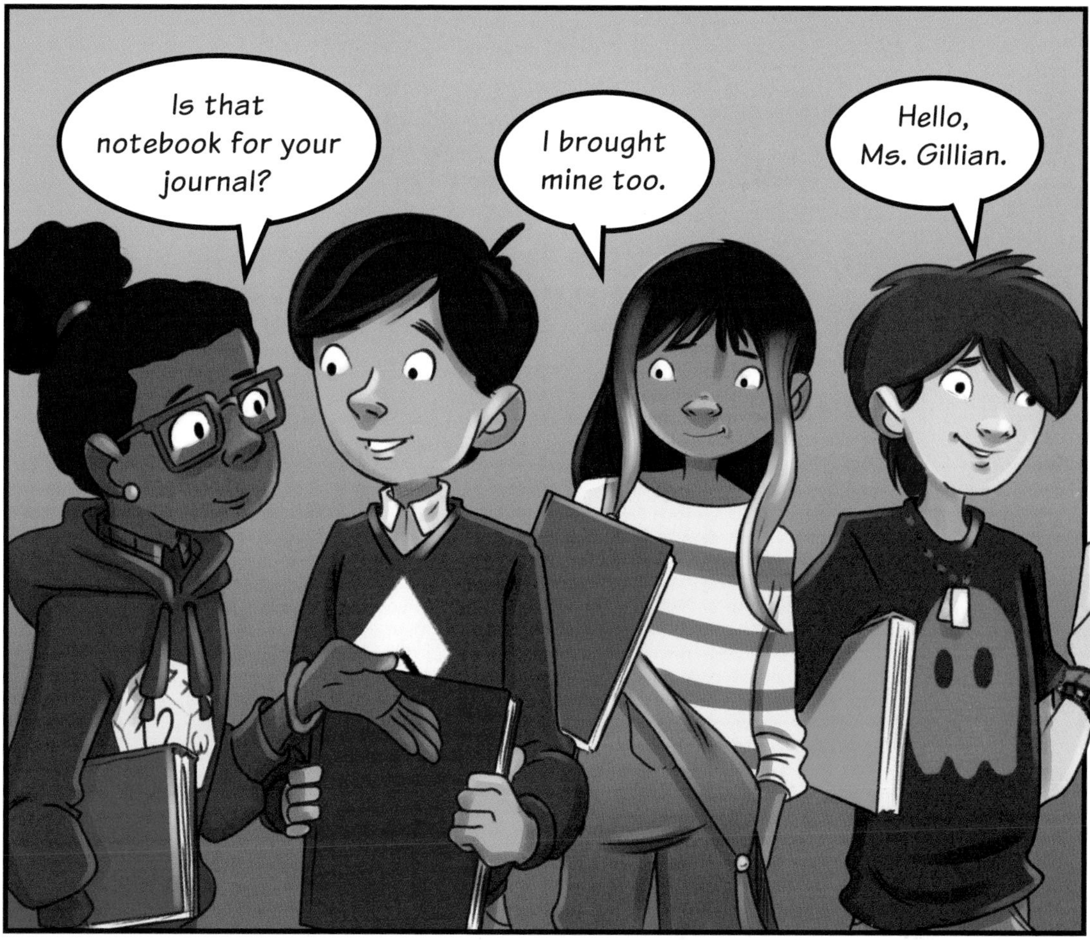
Is that notebook for your journal?
I brought mine too.
Hello, Ms. Gillian.

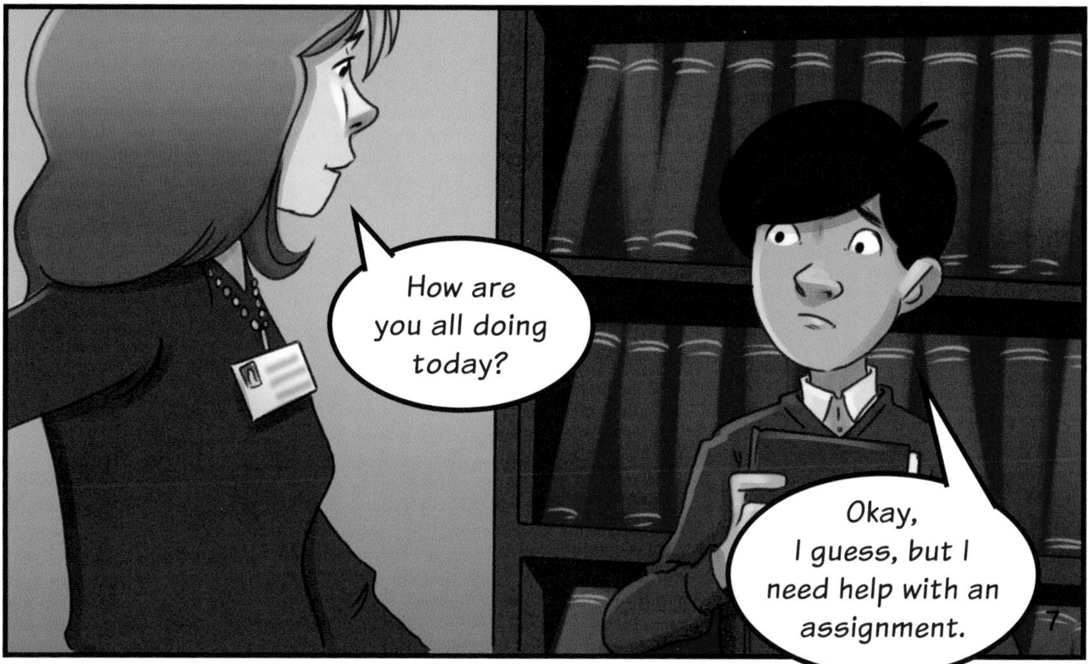
How are you all doing today?
Okay, I guess, but I need help with an assignment.

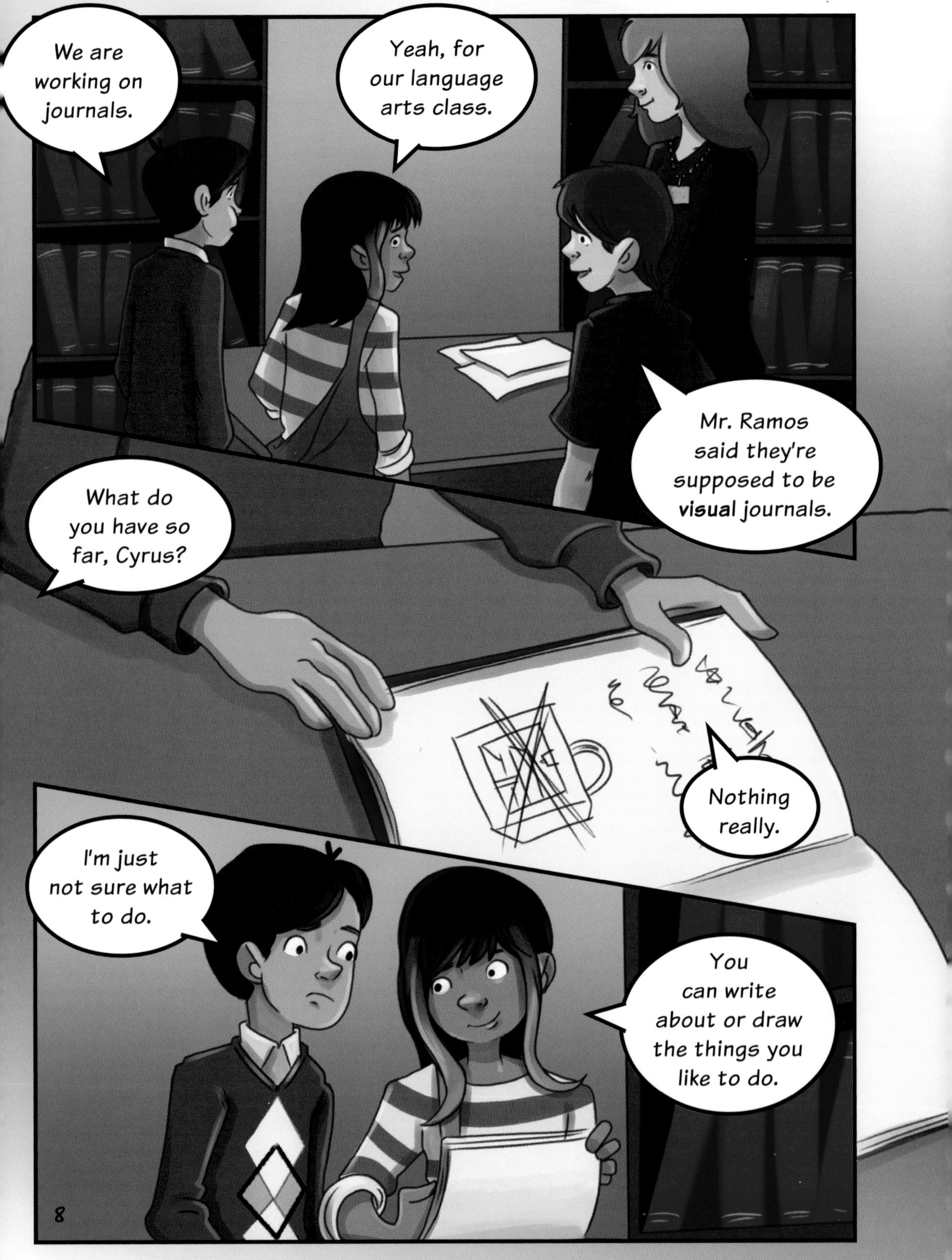
We are working on journals.
Yeah, for our language arts class.
Mr. Ramos said they're supposed to be **visual** journals.
What do you have so far, Cyrus?
Nothing really.
I'm just not sure what to do.
You can write about or draw the things you like to do.

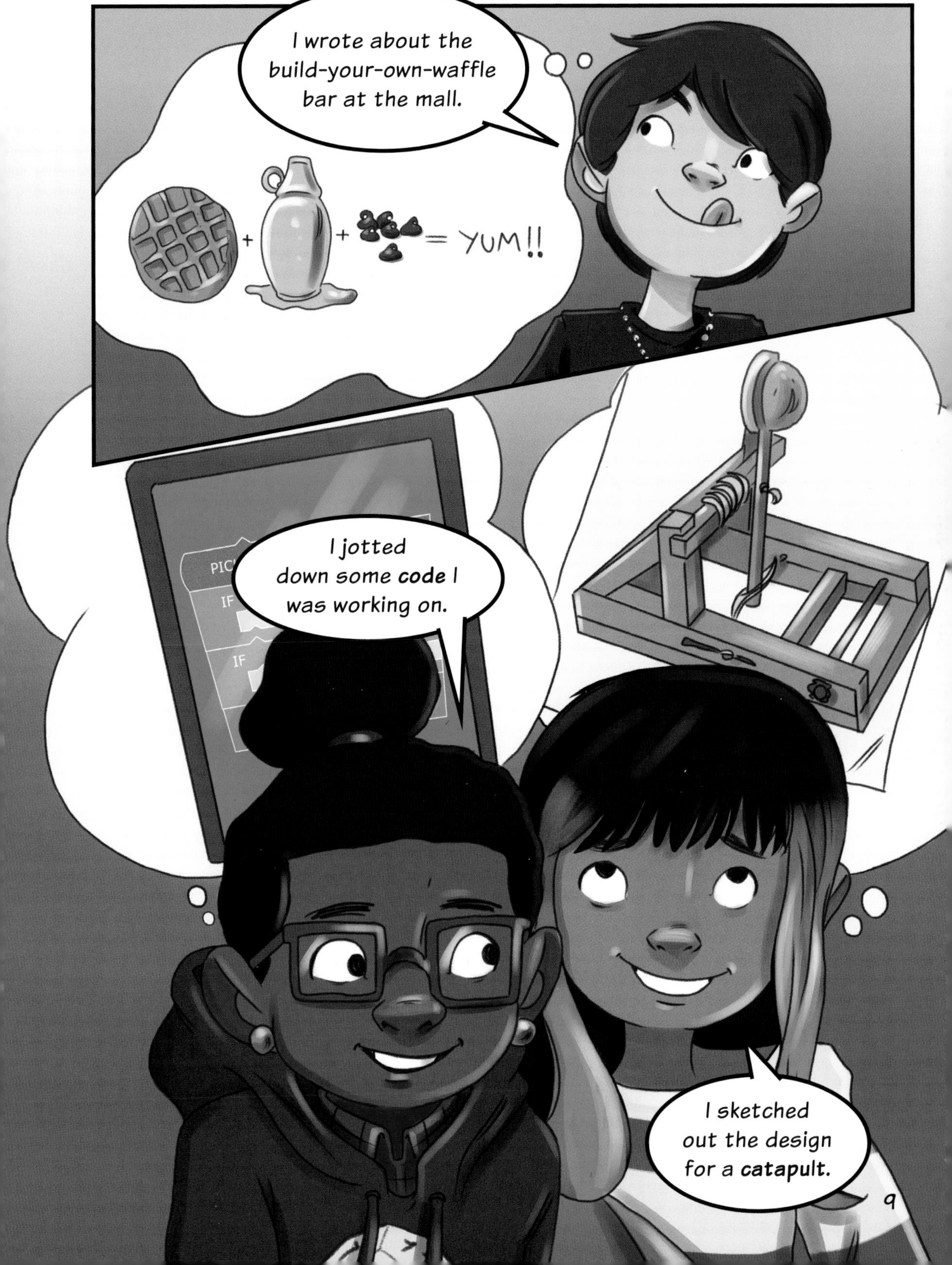

I wrote about the build-your-own-waffle bar at the mall.
+ + = YUM!!
I jotted down some **code** I was working on.
PIC
IF
IF
I sketched out the design for a **catapult.**

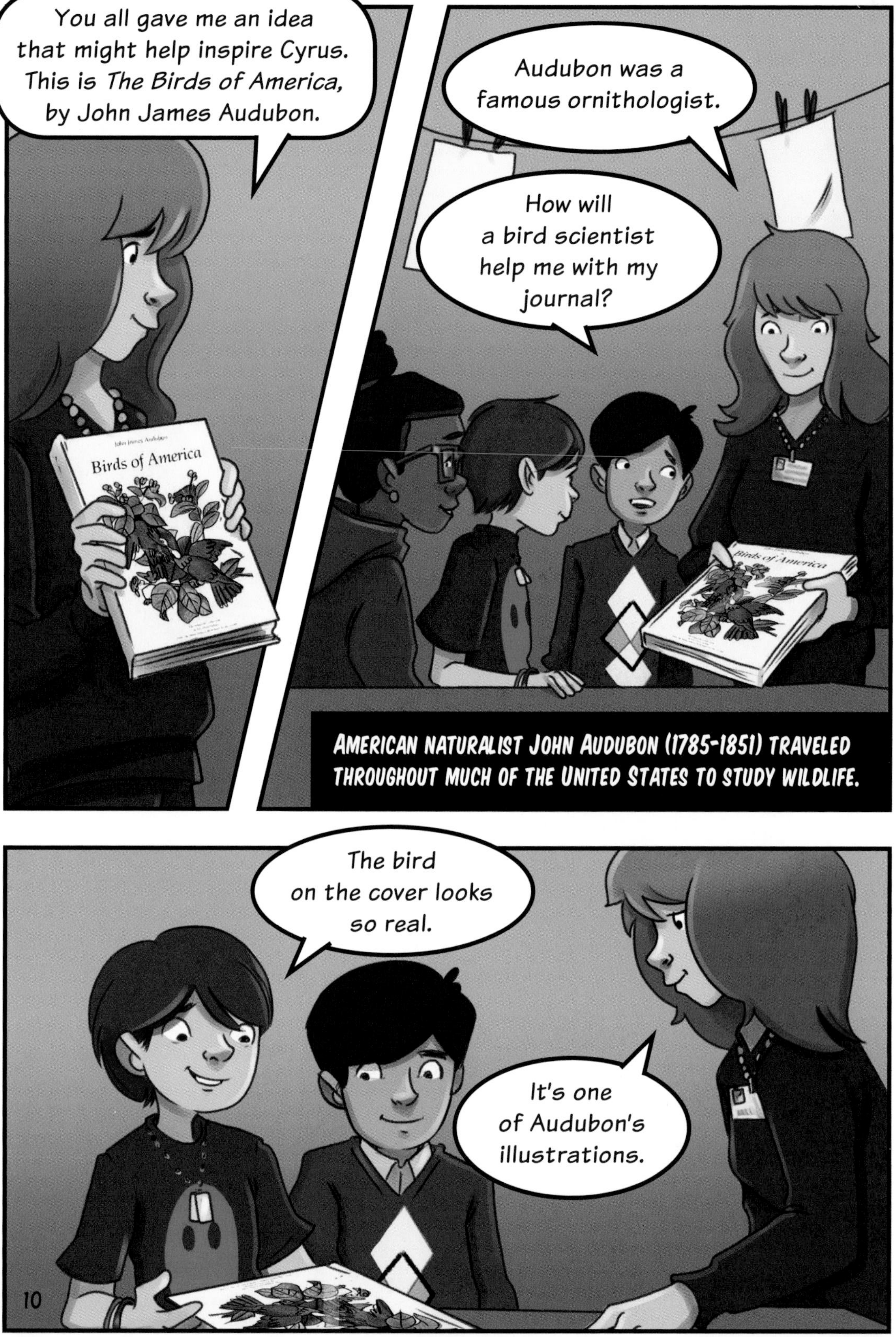

You all gave me an idea that might help inspire Cyrus. This is *The Birds of America,* by John James Audubon.
Birds of America
Audubon was a famous ornithologist.
How will a bird scientist help me with my journal?
Birds of America
AMERICAN NATURALIST JOHN AUDUBON (1785-1851) TRAVELED THROUGHOUT MUCH OF THE UNITED STATES TO STUDY WILDLIFE.
The bird on the cover looks so real.
It's one of Audubon's illustrations.

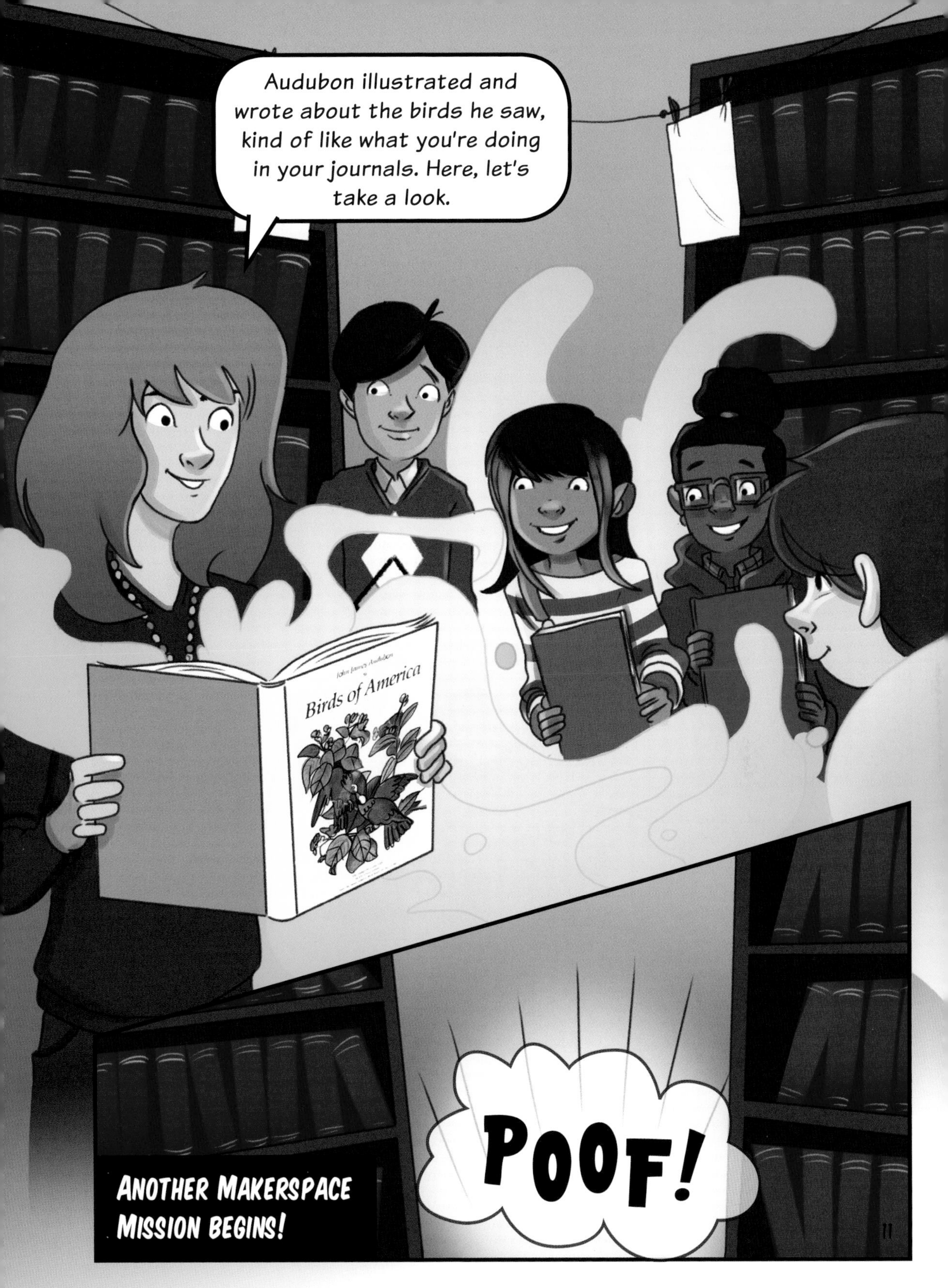
Audubon illustrated and wrote about the birds he saw, kind of like what you're doing in your journals. Here, let's take a look.
John James Audubon
Birds of America
POOF!
ANOTHER MAKERSPACE MISSION BEGINS!

NATURE WALK

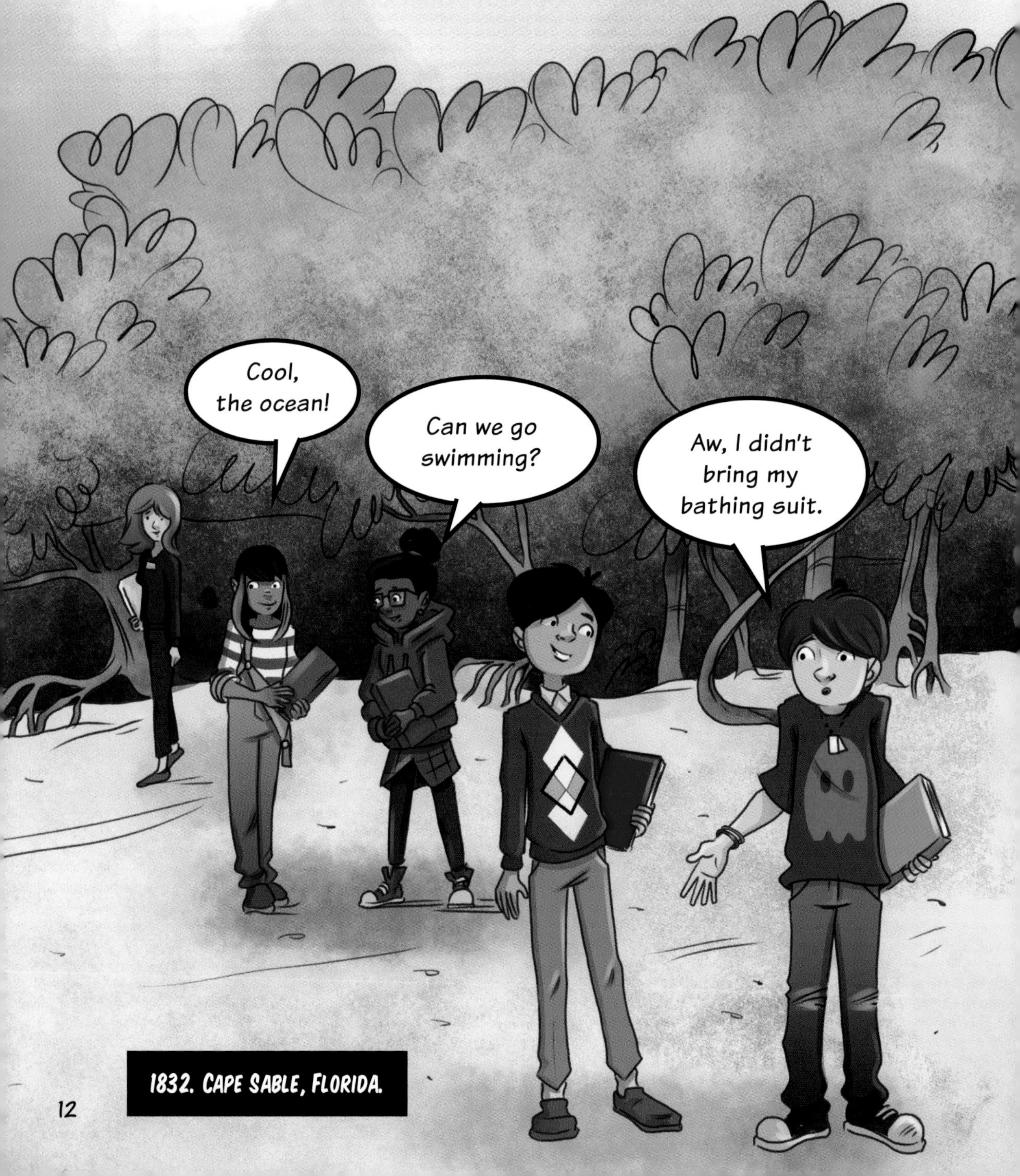
Cool, the ocean!
Can we go swimming?
Aw, I didn't bring my bathing suit.
1832. CAPE SABLE, FLORIDA.

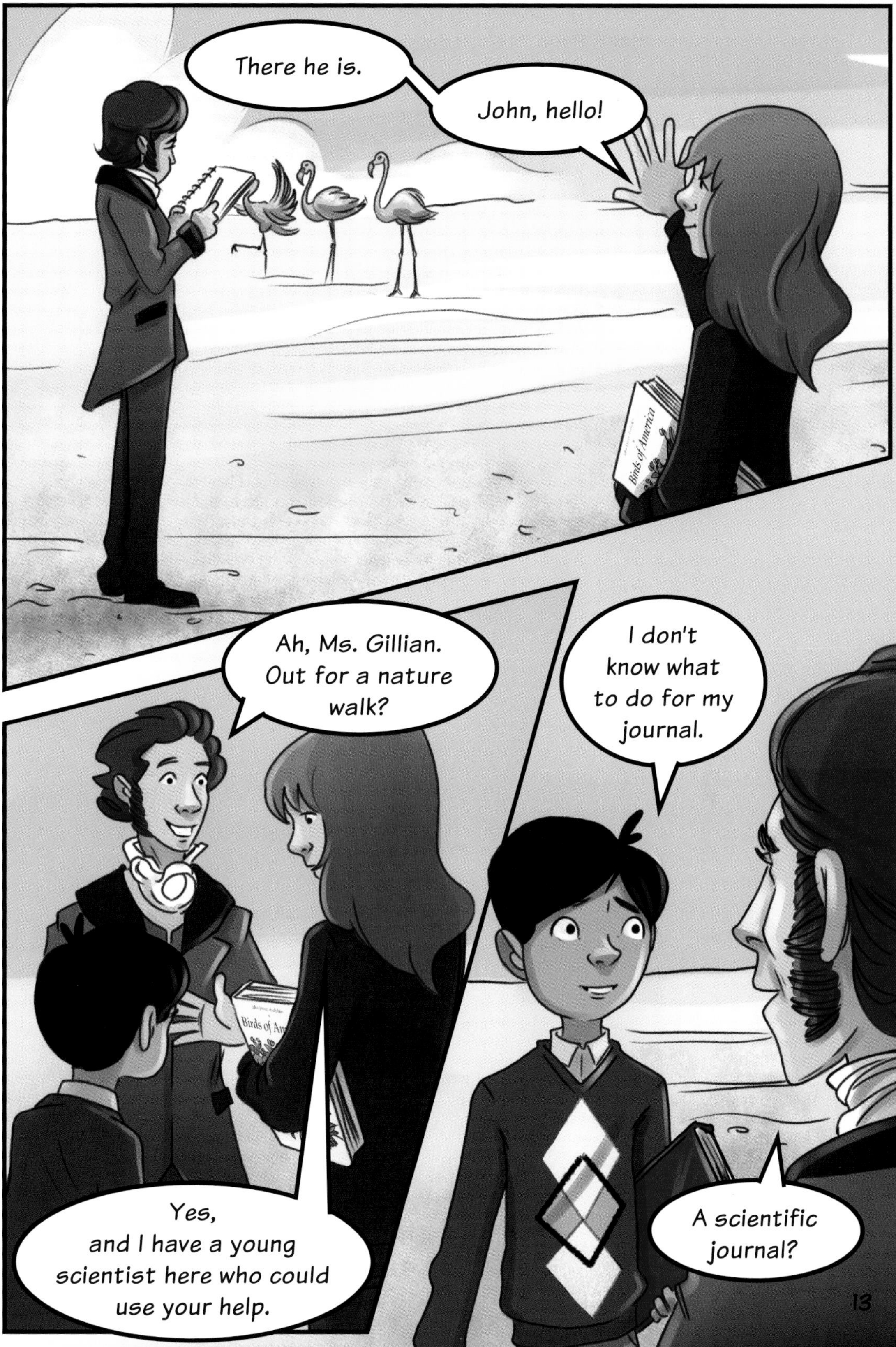
There he is.
John, hello!
Birds of America
Ah, Ms. Gillian. Out for a nature walk?
Yes, and I have a young scientist here who could use your help.
I don't know what to do for my journal.
A scientific journal?

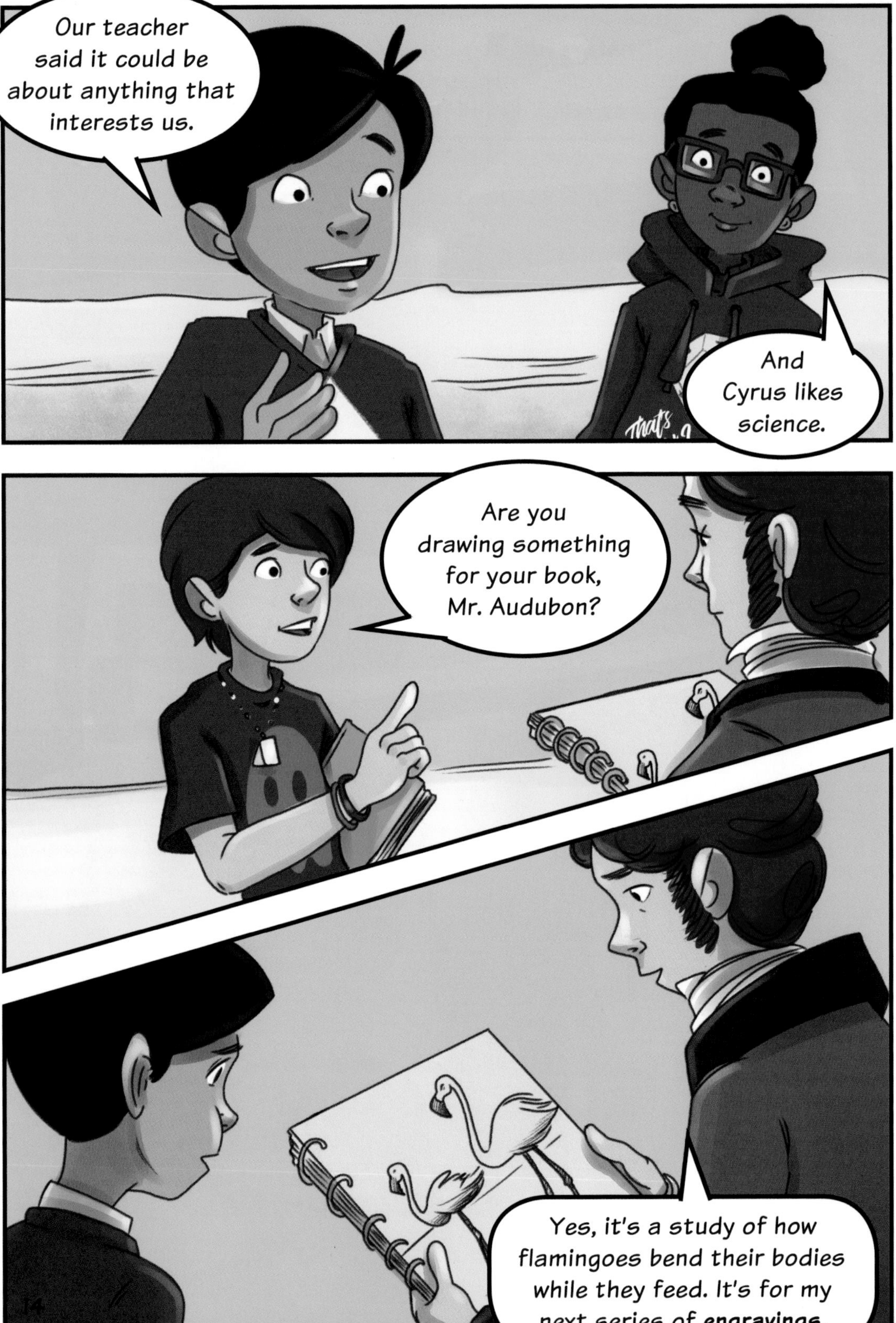
Our teacher said it could be about anything that interests us.
And Cyrus likes science.
Are you drawing something for your book, Mr. Audubon?
Yes, it's a study of how flamingoes bend their bodies while they feed. It's for my next series of **engravings**.

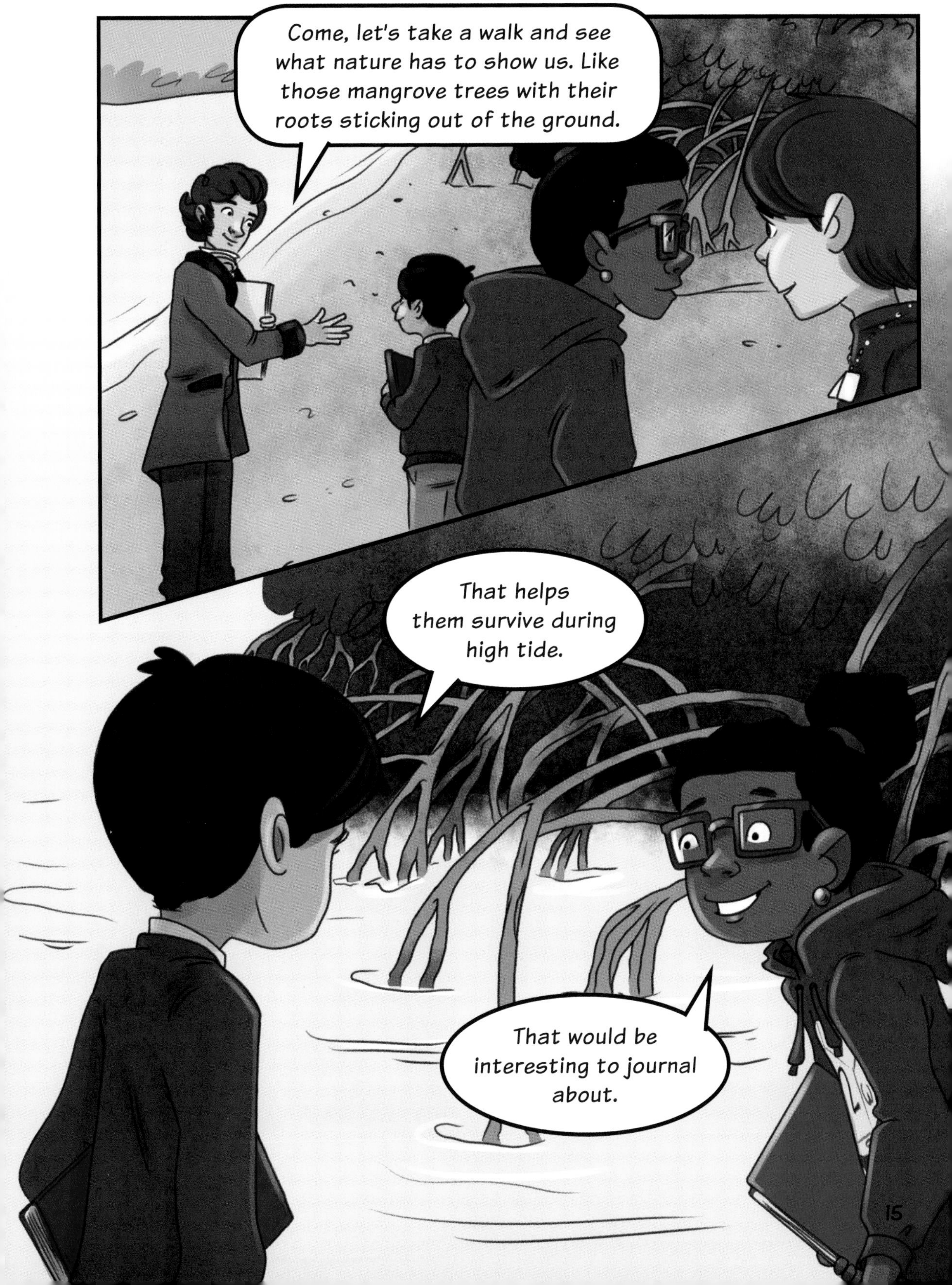
Come, let's take a walk and see what nature has to show us. Like those mangrove trees with their roots sticking out of the ground.
That helps them survive during high tide.
That would be interesting to journal about.

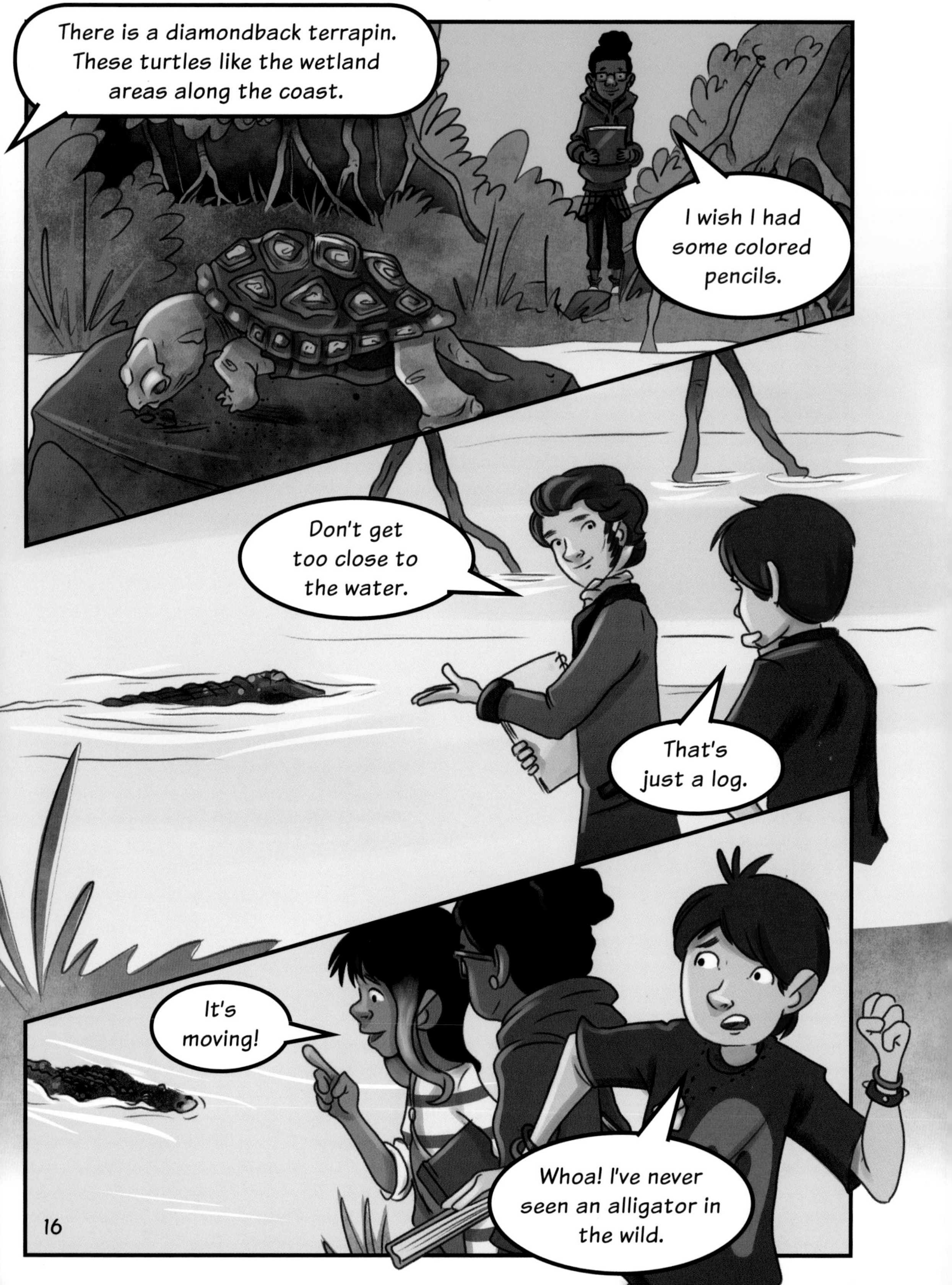
There is a diamondback terrapin. These turtles like the wetland areas along the coast.
I wish I had some colored pencils.
Don't get too close to the water.
That's just a log.
It's moving!
Whoa! I've never seen an alligator in the wild.

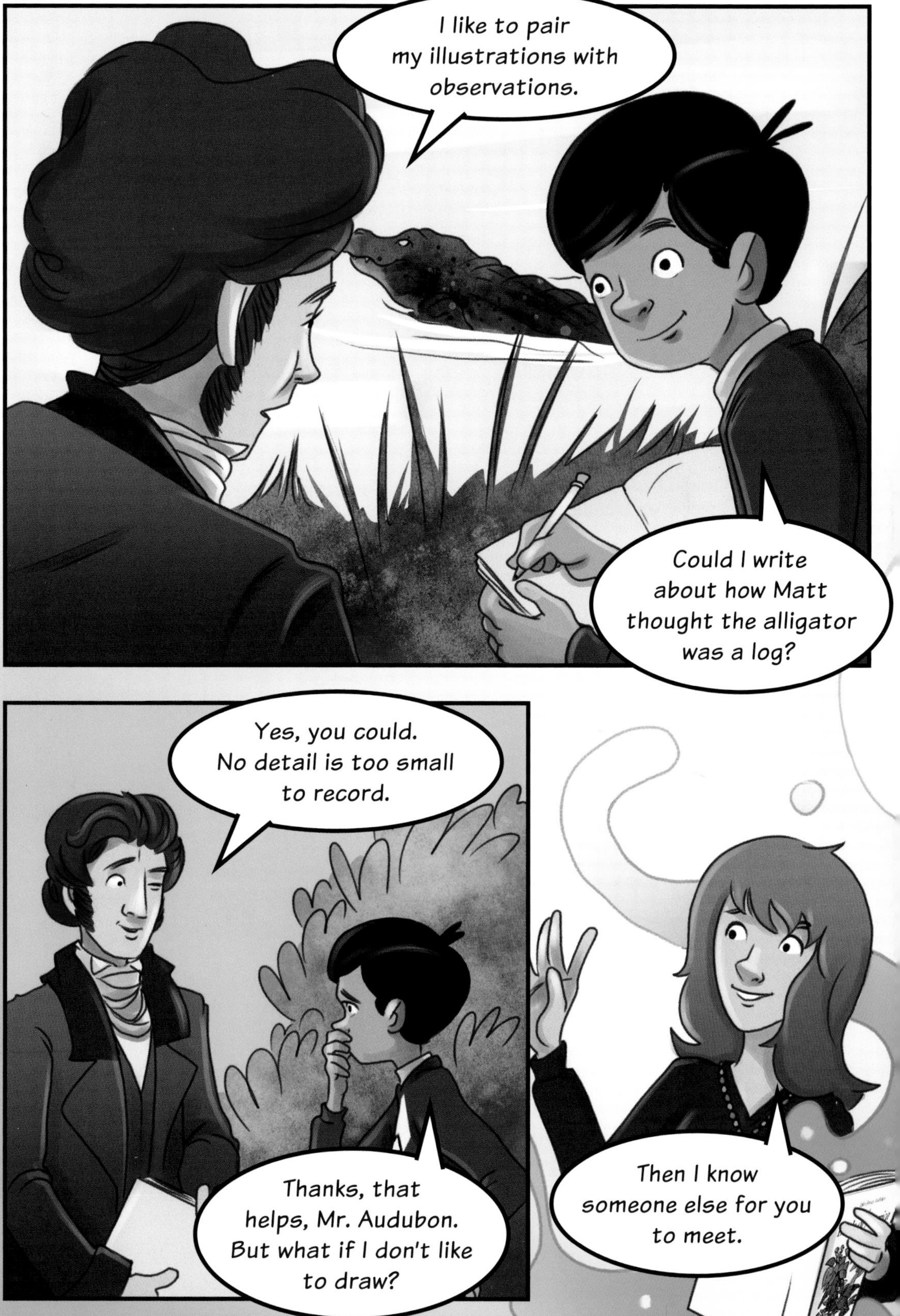
I like to pair my illustrations with observations.
Could I write about how Matt thought the alligator was a log?
Yes, you could. No detail is too small to record.
Thanks, that helps, Mr. Audubon. But what if I don't like to draw?
Then I know someone else for you to meet.

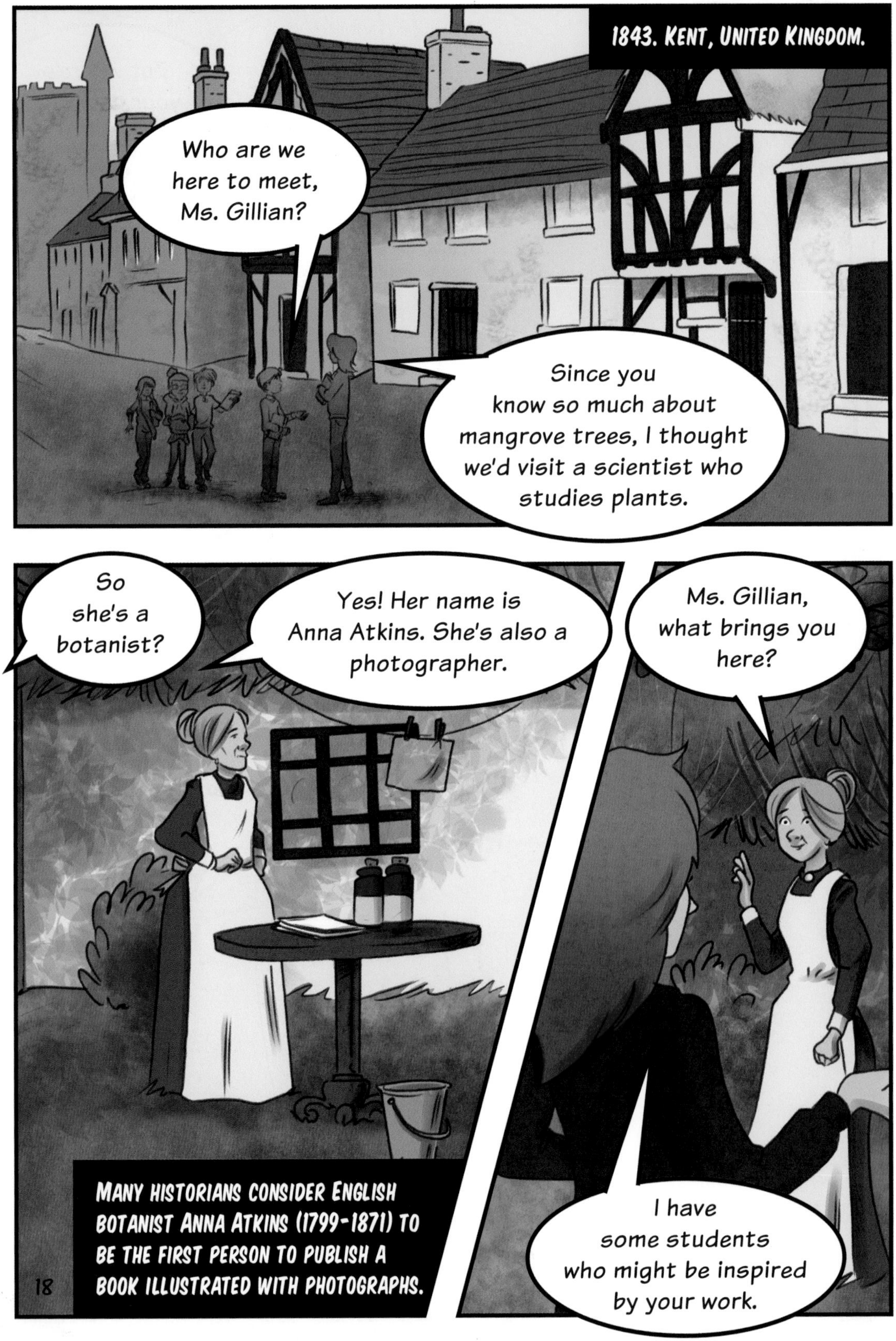
1843. KENT, UNITED KINGDOM.
Who are we here to meet, Ms. Gillian?
Since you know so much about mangrove trees, I thought we'd visit a scientist who studies plants.
So she's a botanist?
Yes! Her name is Anna Atkins. She's also a photographer.
MANY HISTORIANS CONSIDER ENGLISH BOTANIST ANNA ATKINS (1799-1871) TO BE THE FIRST PERSON TO PUBLISH A BOOK ILLUSTRATED WITH PHOTOGRAPHS.
Ms. Gillian, what brings you here?
I have some students who might be inspired by your work.

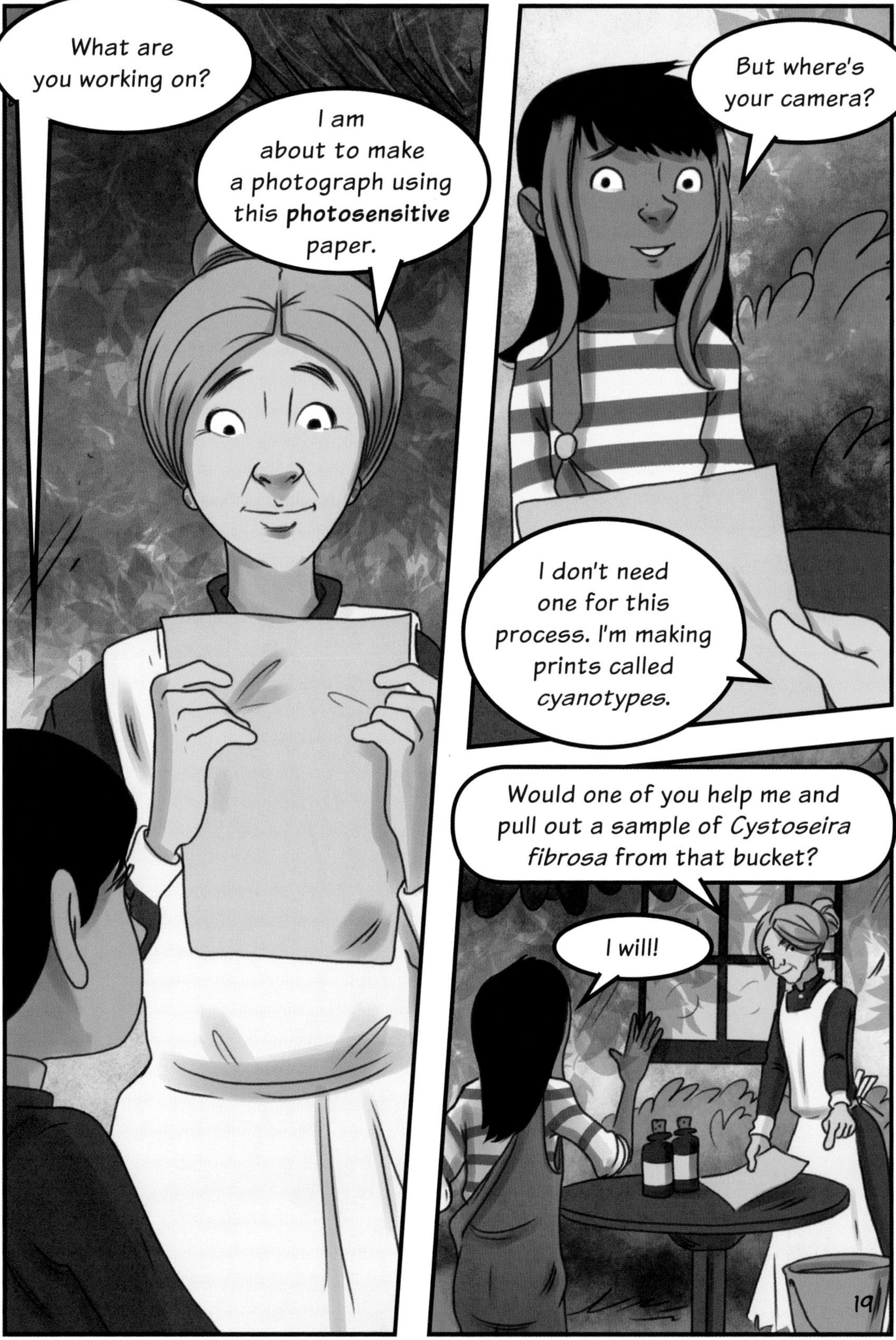
What are you working on?
I am about to make a photograph using this **photosensitive** paper.
But where's your camera?
I don't need one for this process. I'm making prints called *cyanotypes*.
Would one of you help me and pull out a sample of *Cystoseira fibrosa* from that bucket?
I will!

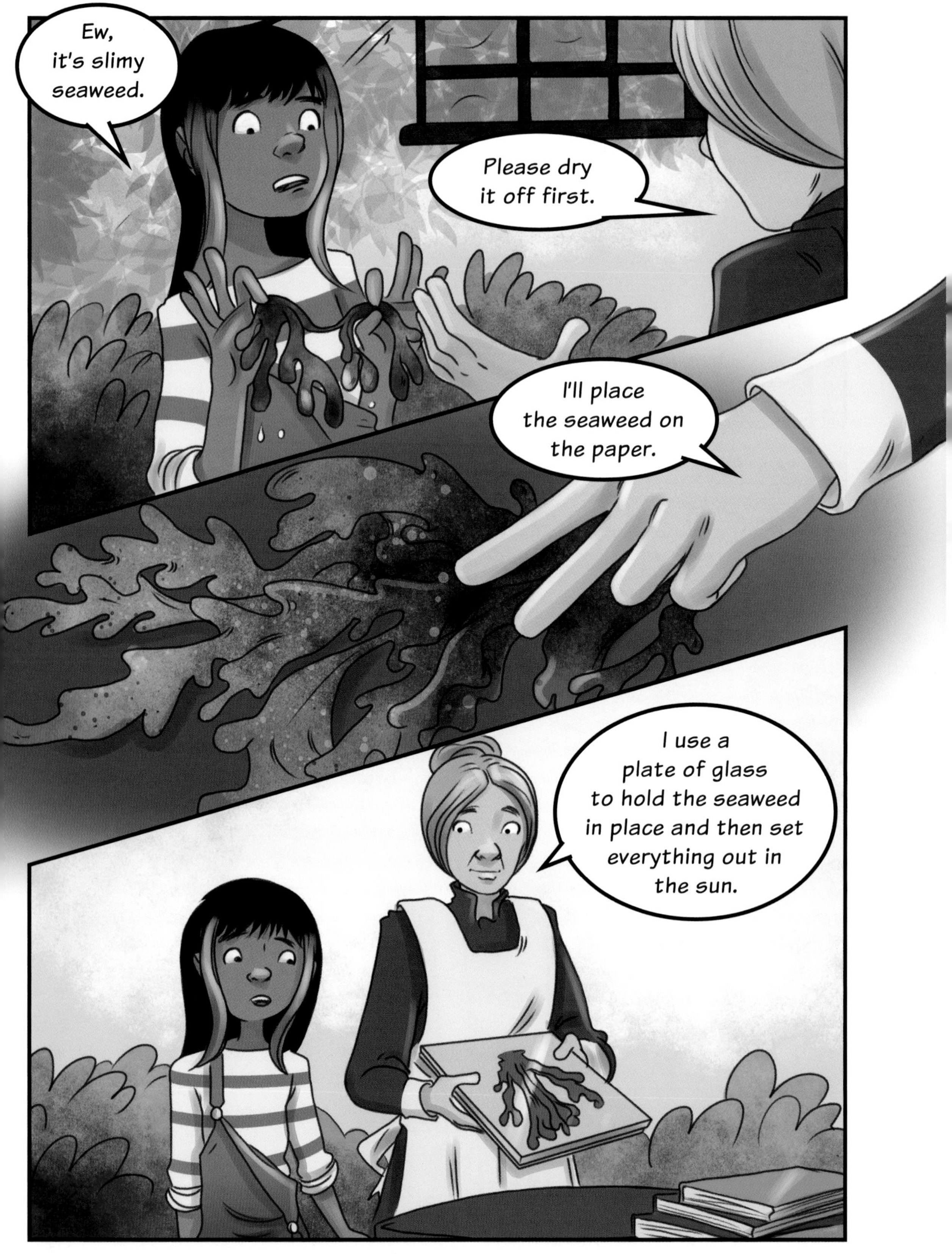
Ew, it's slimy seaweed.
Please dry it off first.
I'll place the seaweed on the paper.
I use a plate of glass to hold the seaweed in place and then set everything out in the sun.

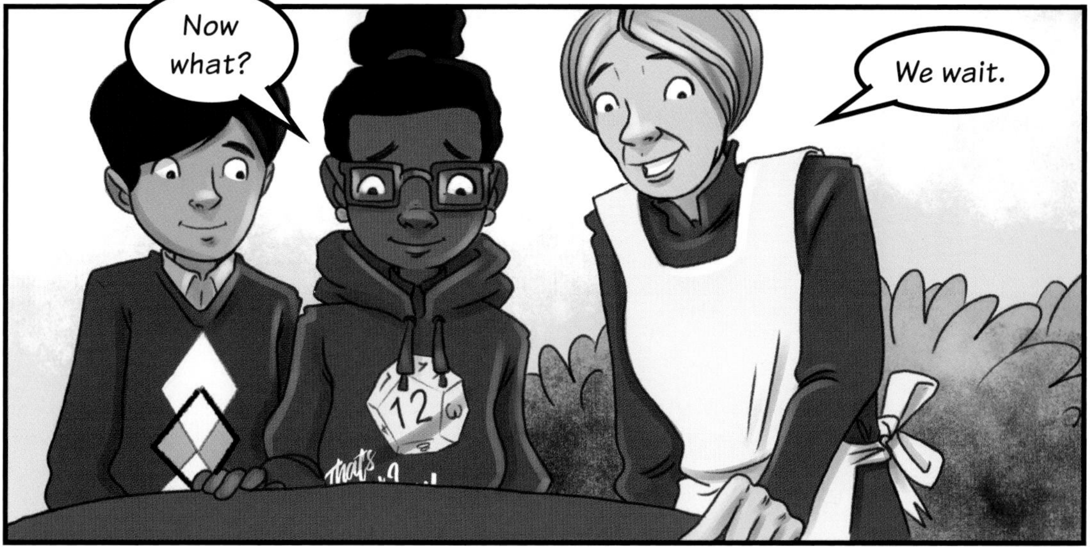
Now what?
We wait.

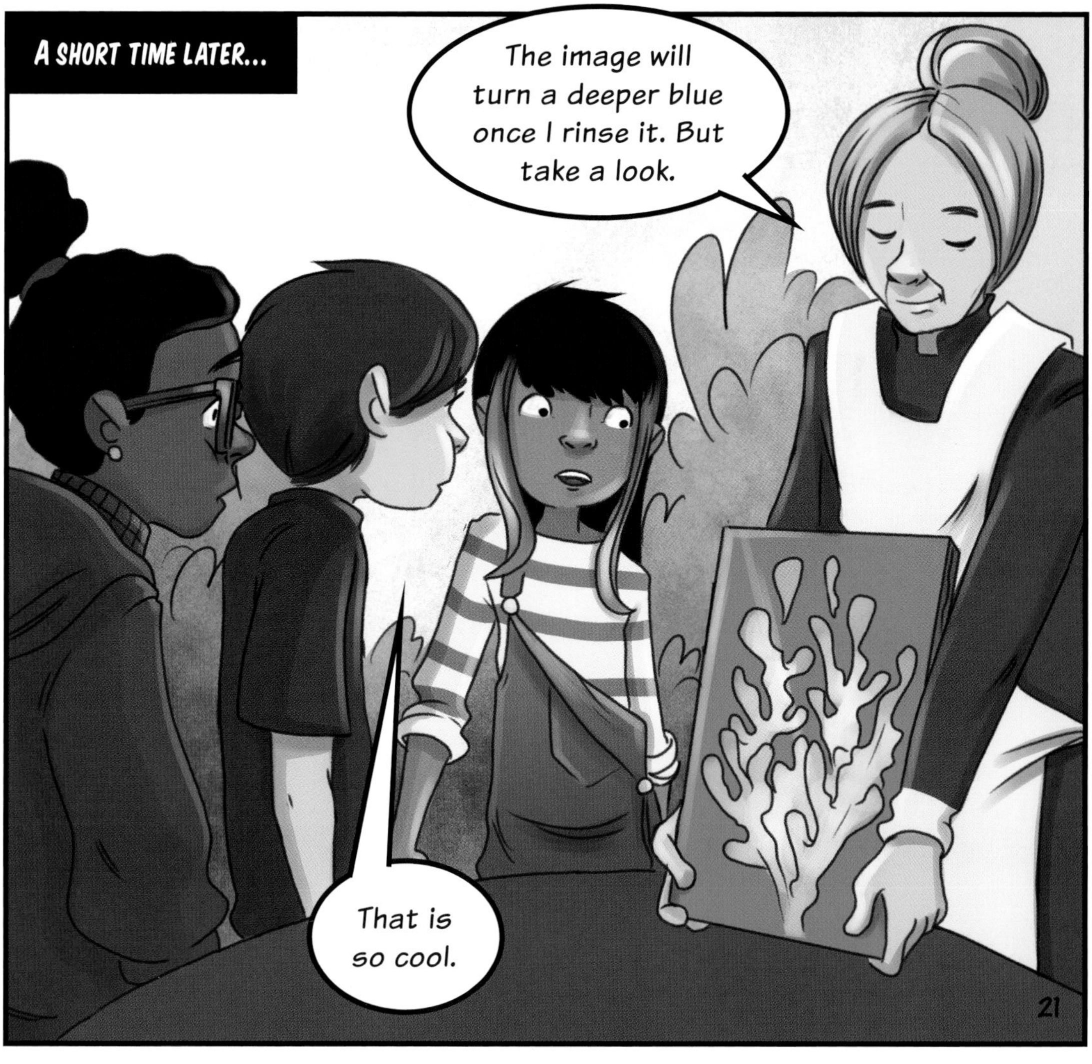
A SHORT TIME LATER...
The image will turn a deeper blue once I rinse it. But take a look.
That is so cool.

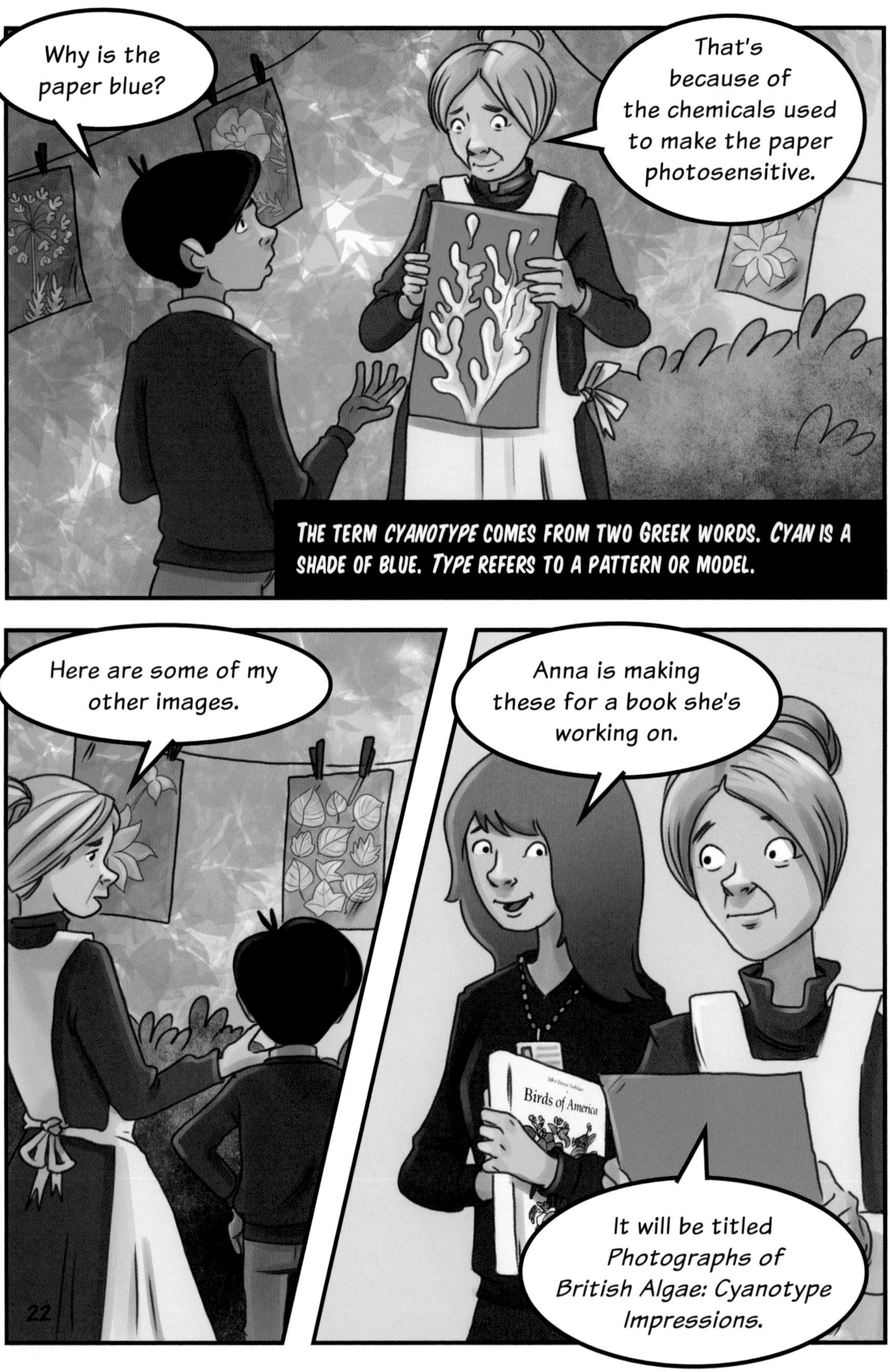
Why is the paper blue?
That's because of the chemicals used to make the paper photosensitive.
THE TERM *CYANOTYPE* COMES FROM TWO GREEK WORDS. *CYAN* IS A SHADE OF BLUE. *TYPE* REFERS TO A PATTERN OR MODEL.
Here are some of my other images.
Anna is making these for a book she's working on.
Birds of America
It will be titled *Photographs of British Algae: Cyanotype Impressions.*

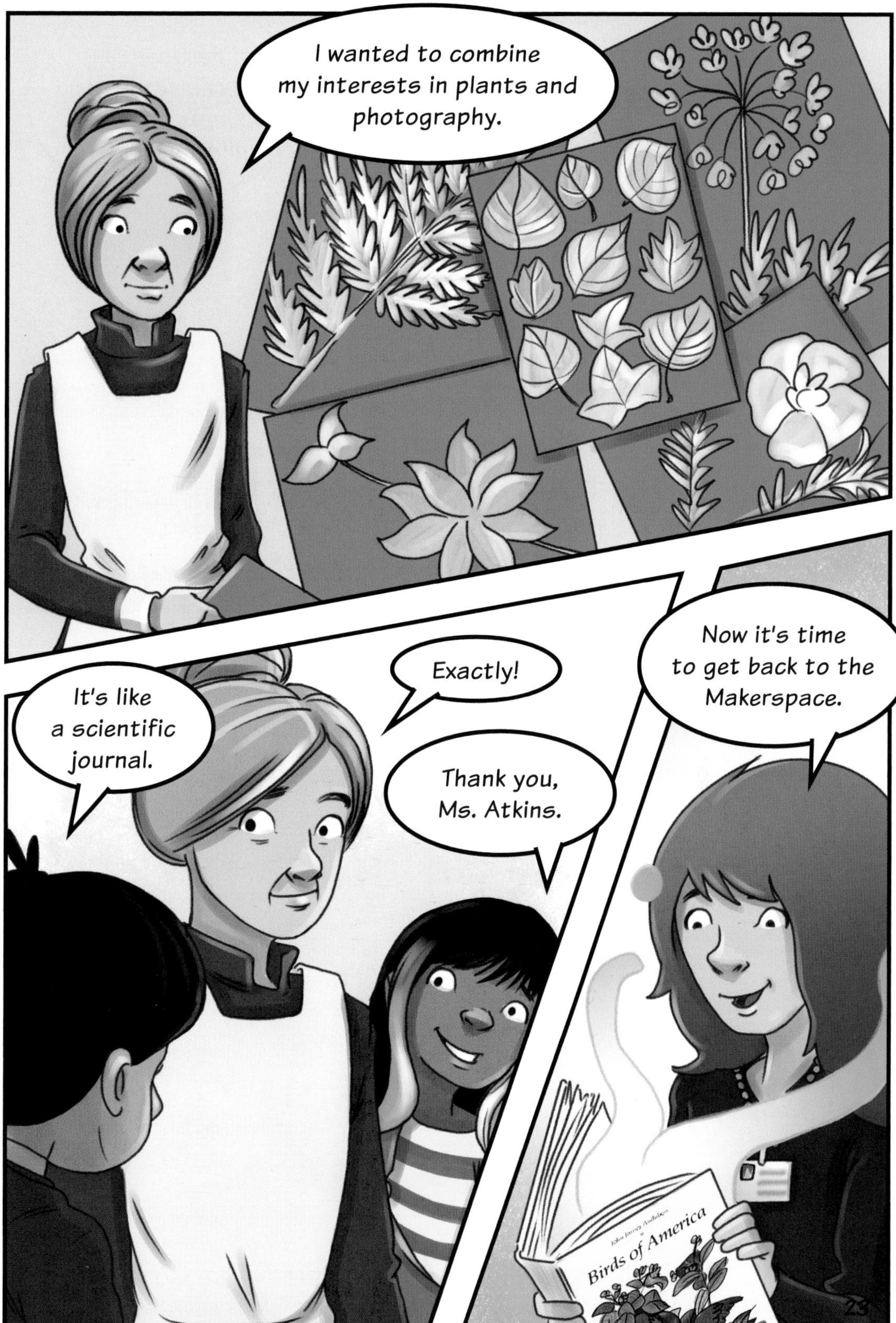
I wanted to combine my interests in plants and photography.
It's like a scientific journal.
Exactly!
Thank you, Ms. Atkins.
Now it's time to get back to the Makerspace.
Birds of America

PHOTO JOURNAL

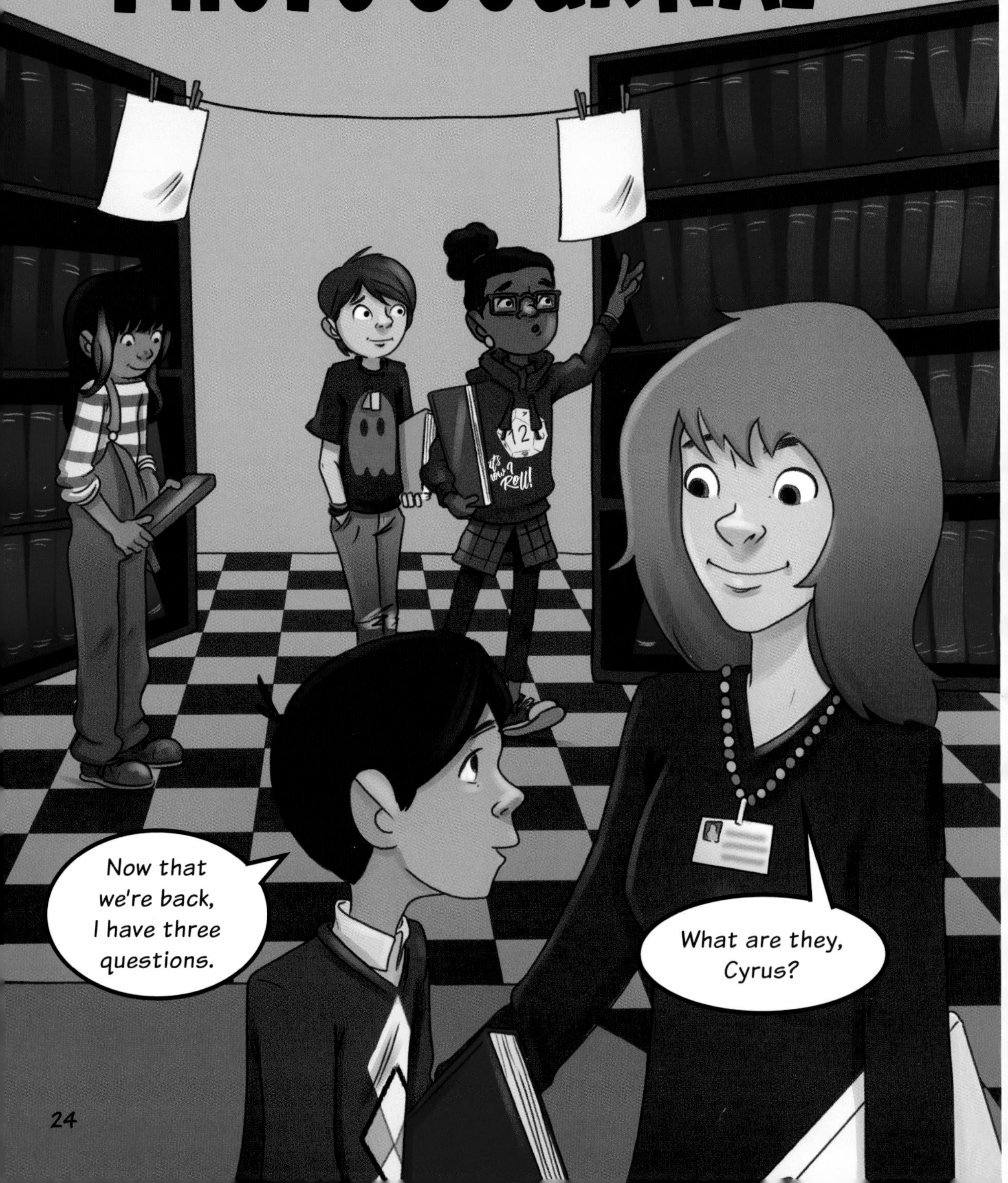

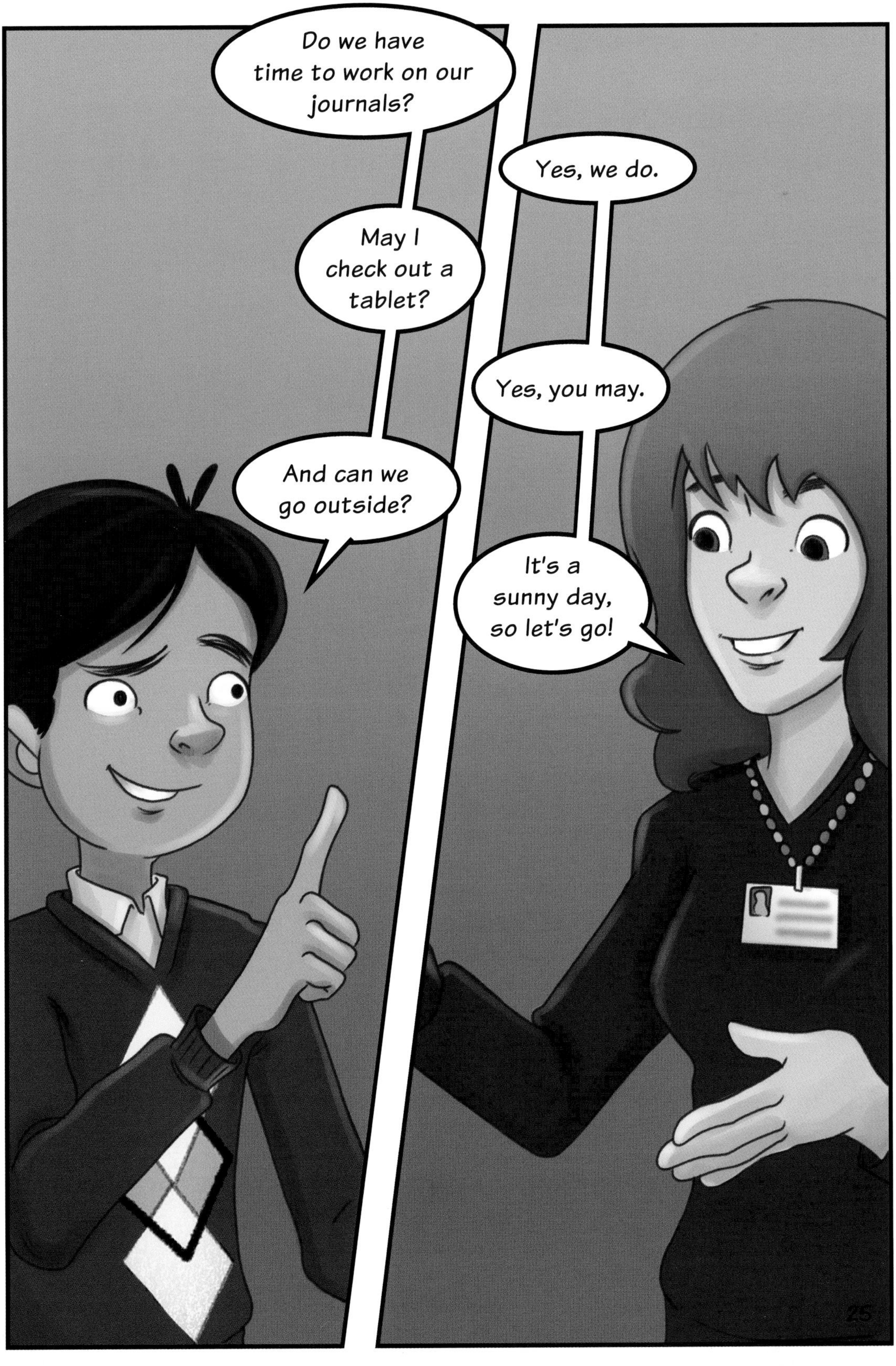
Do we have time to work on our journals?
Yes, we do.
May I check out a tablet?
Yes, you may.
And can we go outside?
It's a sunny day, so let's go!

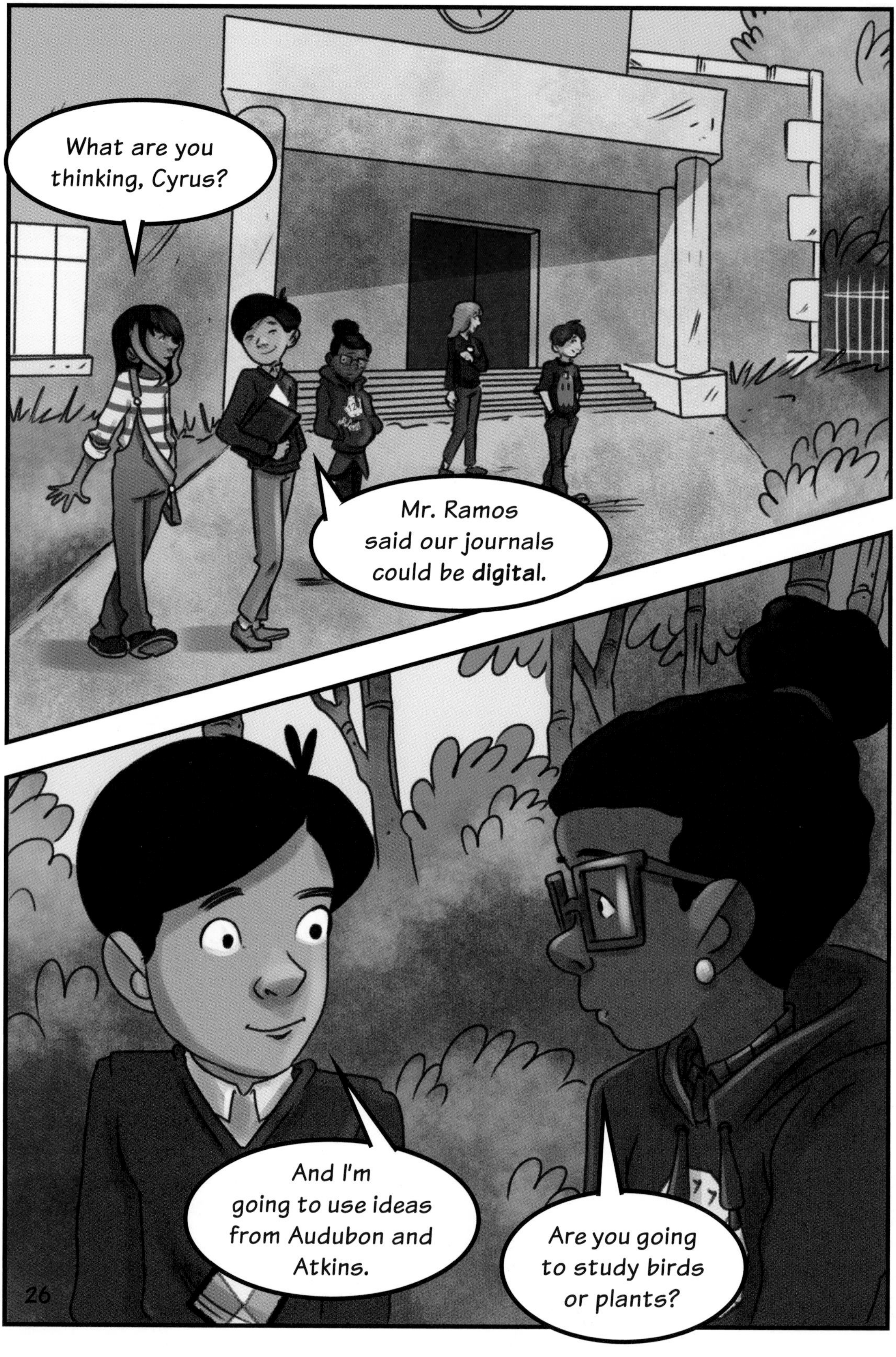
What are you thinking, Cyrus?
Mr. Ramos said our journals could be **digital**.
And I'm going to use ideas from Audubon and Atkins.
Are you going to study birds or plants?

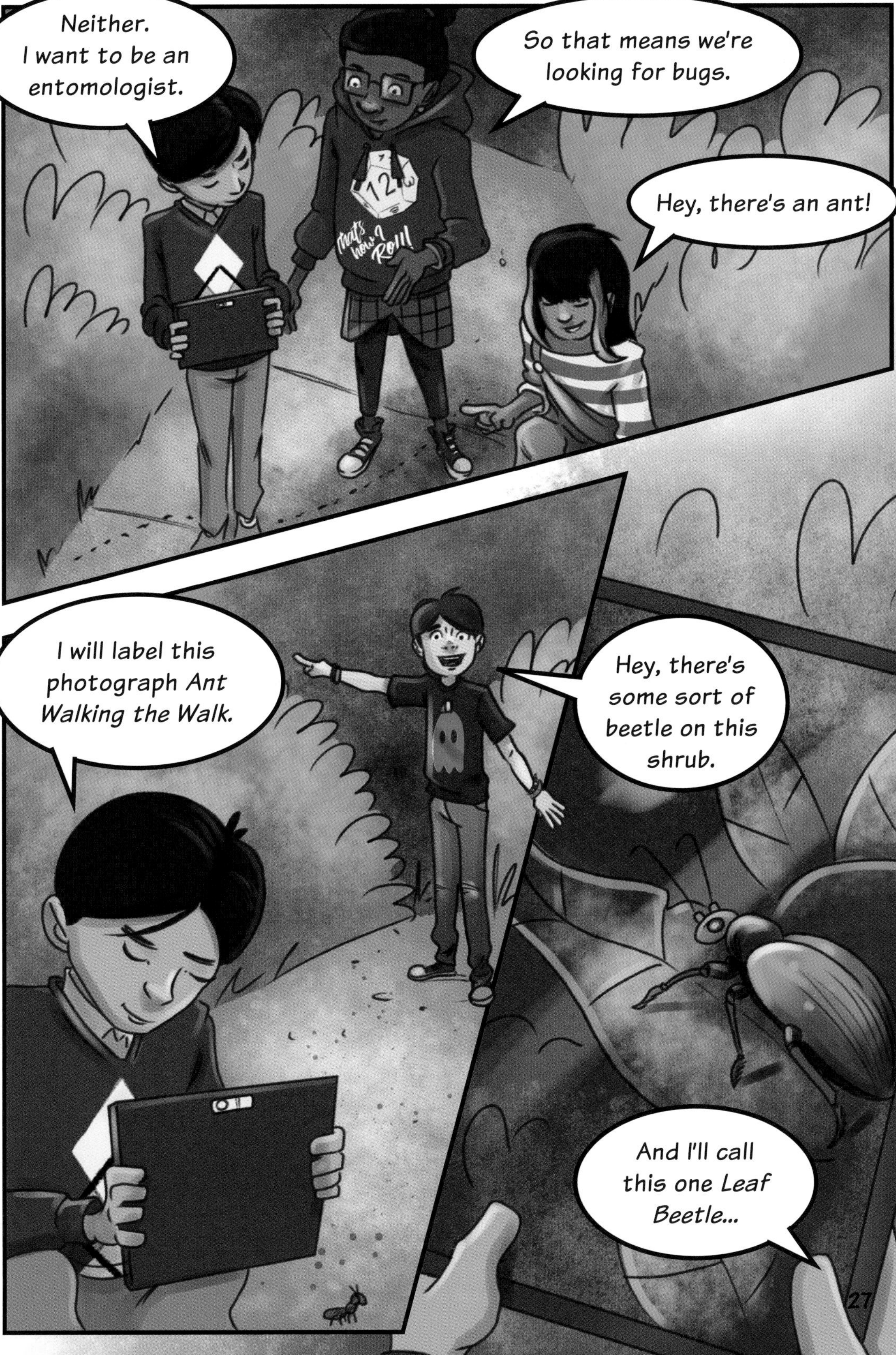
Neither. I want to be an entomologist.
So that means we're looking for bugs.
Hey, there's an ant!
I will label this photograph *Ant Walking the Walk.*
Hey, there's some sort of beetle on this shrub.
And I'll call this one *Leaf Beetle...*

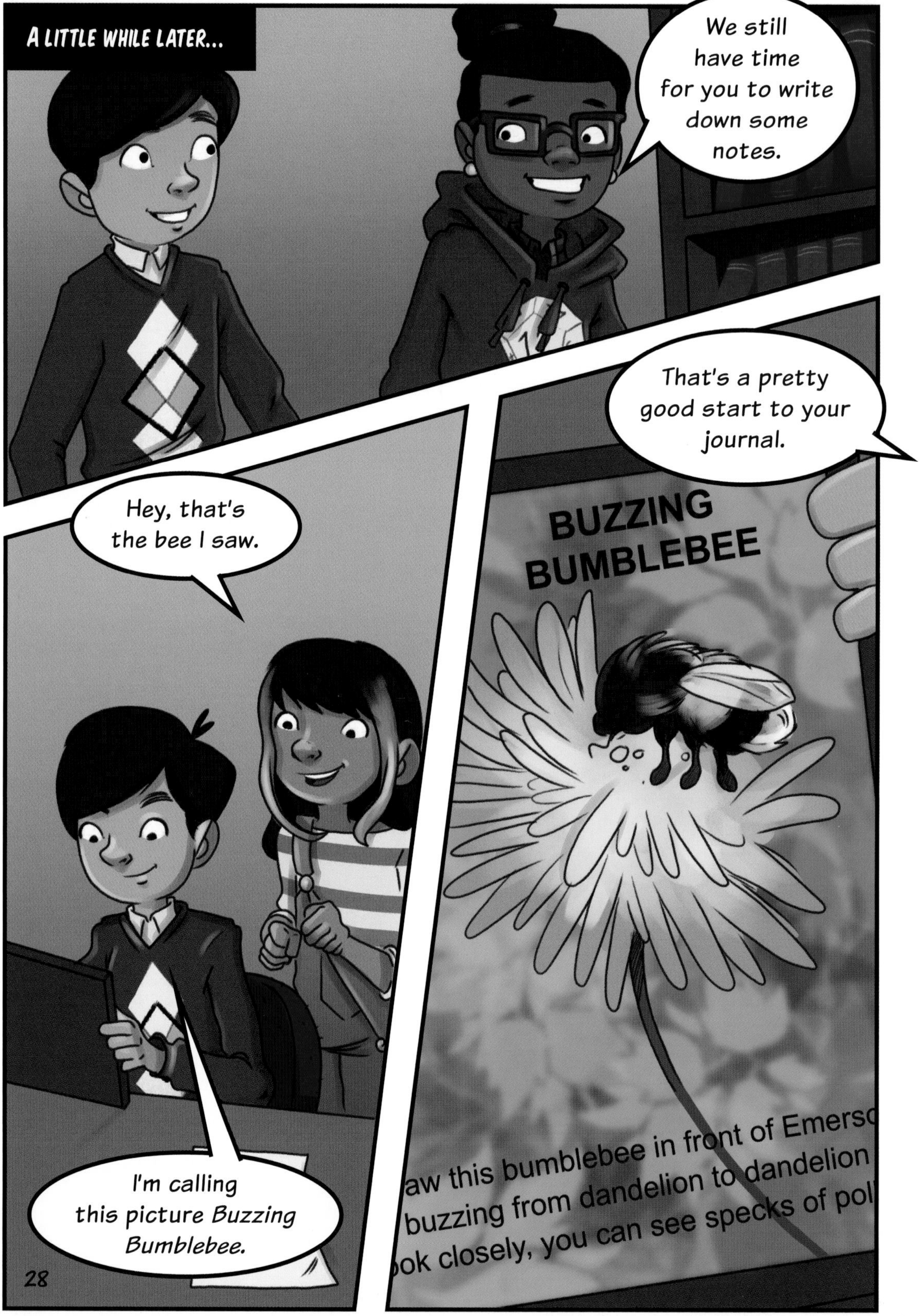
A LITTLE WHILE LATER...
We still have time for you to write down some notes.
Hey, that's the bee I saw.
I'm calling this picture *Buzzing Bumblebee.*
That's a pretty good start to your journal.
BUZZING BUMBLEBEE
aw this bumblebee in front of Emerso
buzzing from dandelion to dandelion
ok closely, you can see specks of pol

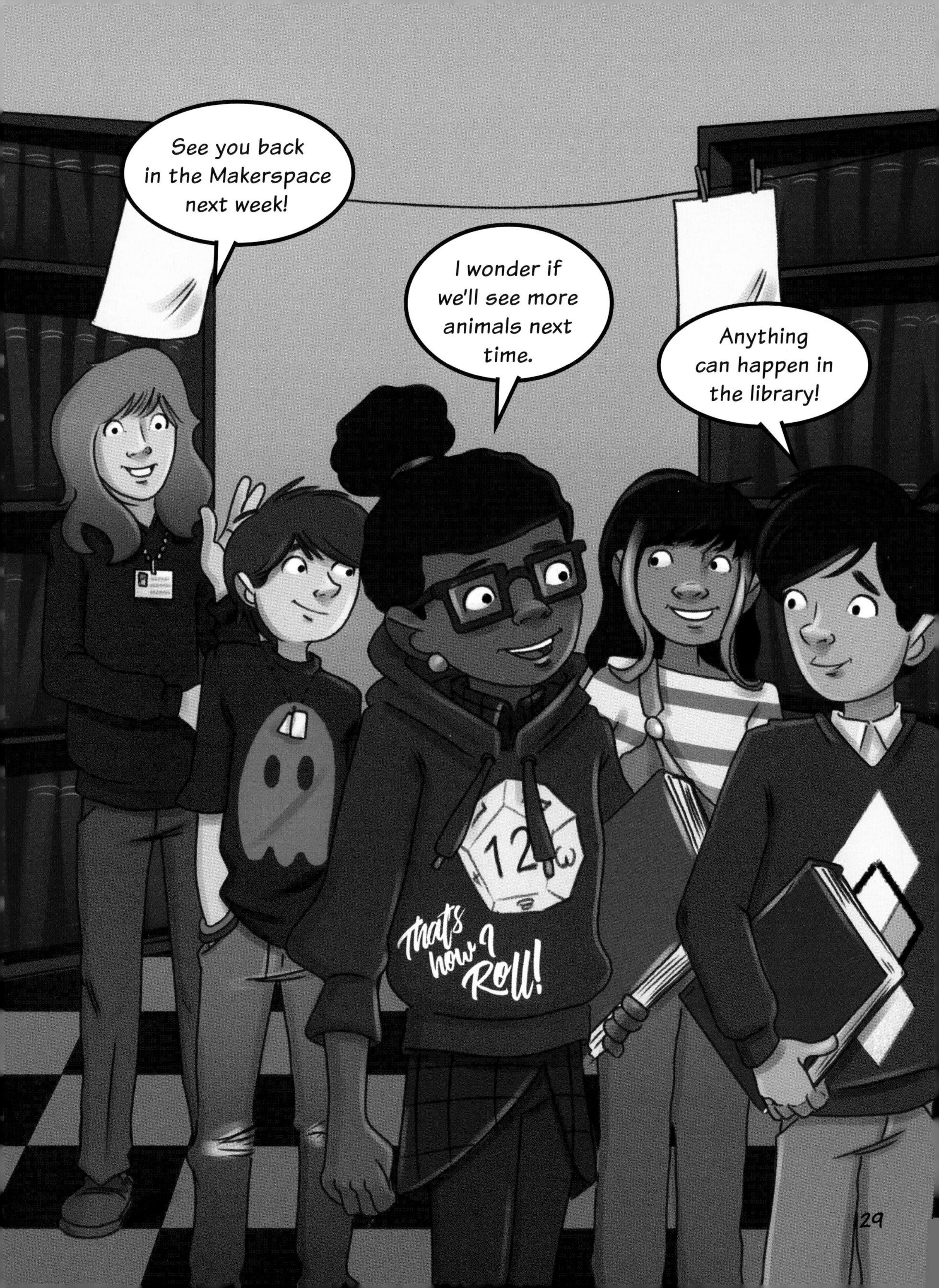
See you back in the Makerspace next week!
I wonder if we'll see more animals next time.
Anything can happen in the library!
12
That's how I Roll!

GLOSSARY

catapult—device for launching objects into the air

code—series of symbols, numbers, and letters that instruct a computer to perform a certain function

digital—electronic

engraving—print made from a surface, such as wood or metal, which has had an image carved into it

photosensitive—sensitive to light

visual—having to do with things seen

CREATE YOUR OWN MAKERSPACE!

1. Find a place to store supplies. It could be a large area, like the space in this story. But it can also be a cart, bookshelf, or storage bin.

2. Make a list of supplies that you would like to have. Include items found in your recycling bin, such as cardboard boxes, tin cans, and plastic bottles (caps too!). Add art materials, household items such as rubber bands, paper clips, straws, and any other materials useful for planning, building, and creating.

3. Pass out your list to friends and parents. Ask them for help in gathering the materials.

4. It's time to create. Let your imagination run wild!

MAKE A PHOTO JOURNAL!

WHAT YOU NEED

- Notebook
- Magazines
- Scissors
- Tape or glue stick
- Pen or pencil

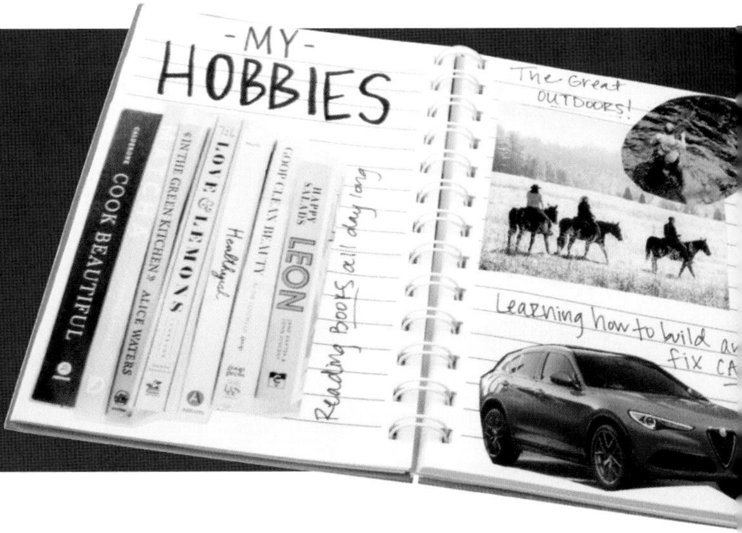

-MY-
HOBBIES
Reading Books all day long
COOK BEAUTIFUL
LOVE & LEMONS
LEON
The Great OUTDOORS!

1. ***Pick your topic.*** *Decide what you would like to create a journal about. It could be fashion, animals, technology, or anything else that interests you. You can pick more than one topic, too.*
2. ***Search for photos.*** *Look through the magazines, searching for photos and other images that fit your interest. Cut them out.*
3. ***Create your journal.*** *Tape or glue the images you selected onto pages of the notebook.*
4. ***Add notes.*** *Next to each image, write your personal observations. You can describe what's in the image or write what you think about it. Note what you know about the subject of the image. You could even make up a story about it!*

FURTHER RESOURCES

Johnson, Robin. *Everglades Research Journal.* New York: Crabtree, 2018.

McFadzean, Lesley. *Birds: Flying High.* New York: PowerKids Press, 2015.

Miller, Shannon McClintock, and Blake Hoena. *A Robotics Mission.* North Mankato, MN: Capstone, 2019.

Robinson, Fiona. *The Bluest of Blues: Anna Atkins and the First Book of Photographs.* New York: Abrams Books for Young Readers, 2018.

DON'T MISS THESE EXCITING ADVENTURES IN MAKERSPACE!

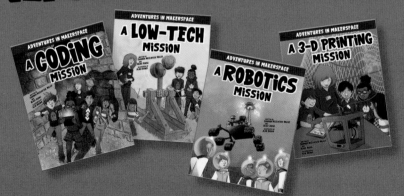